WE'RE GOING ON A LION HUNT

Adapted by
Margery Cuyler

Illustrated by
Joe Mathieu

Marshall Cavendish Children

Text copyright © 2008 by Margery Cuyler
Illustrations copyright © 2008 by Joe Mathieu

All rights reserved
Marshall Cavendish Corporation
99 White Plains Road, Tarrytown, NY 10591
www.marshallcavendish.us/kids

Library of Congress Cataloging-in-Publication Data
Cuyler, Margery.
We're going on a lion hunt / adapted by Margery Cuyler ;
illustrated by Joe Mathieu.
p. cm.
Summary: A class of kindergarteners set out bravely in search of a lion,
going through mud, long grass, and other obstacles before the inevitable
encounter with the lion forces a headlong retreat.
ISBN 978-0-7614-5454-0
[1. Play—Fiction. 2. Imagination—Fiction. 3. Hunting—Fiction. 4.
Lions—Fiction.] I. Mathieu, Joseph, ill. II. Title. III. Title: We are
going on a lion hunt.
PZ7.C997Wc 2008
[E]—dc22
2008003663

The artwork was rendered with Prismacolor pencils
and Luna watercolors on Lanaquarelle paper.
Book design by Vera Soki

Printed in China
First edition
1 3 5 6 4 2

For Juliana and Dick Fenn
—M.C.

To my beautiful granddaughter, Bella
—J.M.

Get ready! We're going on a lion hunt. Time to put on your safari hats. Time to use your imagination.

Lion

We're going on a lion hunt.
We're going to catch a big one.

We're not afraid.
Look what's up ahead!

Mud!
Can't go over it.
Can't go under it.

Can't go around it.
Have to go through it.
Slog, slog, slog.

We're going on a lion hunt.
We're going to catch a big one.
We're not afraid.
Look what's up ahead!

Sticks!
Can't go over them.
Can't go under them.
Can't go around them.
Have to go through them.
Snap, snap, snap.

We're going on a lion hunt.
We're going to catch a big one.
We're not afraid.
Look what's up ahead!

Trees!
Can't go over them.
Can't go under them.
Can't go around them.
Have to climb up them.
Up we go, up we go, up we go.

We're going on a lion hunt.
We're going to catch a big one.
We're not afraid.
Look what's up ahead!
River!

Can't go over it.
Can't go under it.
Can't go around it.
Have to go through it.
Splish-splash, splish-splash, splish-splash.

We're going on a lion hunt.
We're going to catch a big one.
We're not afraid.
Look what's up ahead!
Grass!

Can't go over it.
Can't go under it.
Can't go around it.
Have to go through it.
Swish, swish, swish.

We're going on a lion hunt.
We're going to catch a big one.
We're not afraid.
Look what's up ahead!
Cave!

Can't go over it.
Can't go under it.
Can't go around it.
Have to go through it.
We're not afraid.

OOoo-oooO.

It's dark in here.
We see two shining lights.
We feel something furry.
We feel a c-c-c-cold nose.
We feel s-s-s-sharp teeth.

It's a lion!
Run out of the cave.

Crawl through the grass.

Swim across the river.

Climb up the trees.

Jump through the sticks.

Slosh through the mud.

Run into the school.
Close the door.

Safe at last!